characters created by lauren

I really ABSOLUTELY must have glasses

Text based on the script written by Bridget Hurst

Illustrations from the TV animation produced by Tiger Aspect

PUFFIN BOOKS
Published by the Penguin Group: London, New York, Australia,
Canada, India, Ireland, New Zealand and South Africa
Penguin Books Ltd, Registered Offices: 80 Strand, London WC2R 0RL, England

puffinbooks.com

This edition published in Great Britain in Puffin Books 2010
1 3 5 7 9 8 6 4 2
Text and illustrations copyright © Lauren Child / Tiger Aspect Productions Limited, 2009
The Charlie and Lola Logo is a trademark of Lauren Child
All rights reserved. The moral right of the author/illustrator has been asserted
Manufactured in China
ISBN: 978-0-141-33498-1
This edition produced for The Book People Ltd,
Hall Wood Avenue, Haydock, St Helens, WA11 9UL

I have this little sister Lola.
          She is small and very funny.
Lola is thinking about seeing
          because tomorrow Mum is taking her
to the **optician's** to have her **eyes** tested.

Lola says,
        "But my **eyes** do
not need testing, Charlie."

So I say,
        "But going to
the **optician** is fun.
        You get to find
                hidden pictures
in lots and lots
        of coloured dots."

And Lola says,
        "Dots, Charlie?
        I love dots!"

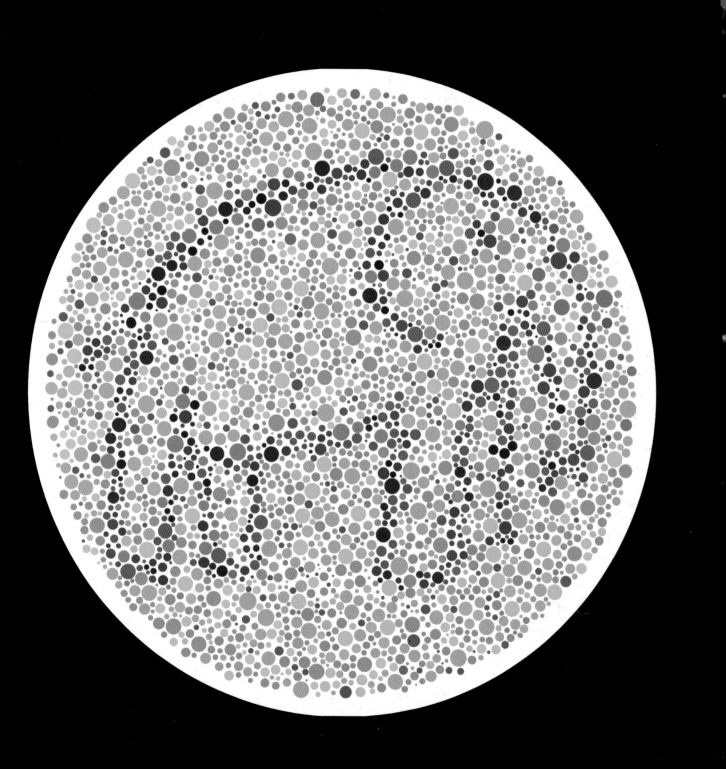

Lola says,
"I can actually
see very well.
I can see my spaghetti,
and my bowl,
and my spoon,
and my pink milk.
AND I can see YOU!

So I really absolutely
do not need to go
to the eye test lady."

At school,
Lola says, "Look!
Mini's got glasses!"

So Lotta asks Mini,
 "Where did you get
your glasses?"

 And Lola says,
"They are especially
 very nice and flowery!"

And Mini says,
 "I went to the optician.
 She said that I
need glasses because
 everything I see
 is slightly fuzzy."

Later on, Lola says,
"Charlie, I can't wait
to go to
the eye test lady!
I am going to get
some flowery glasses."

So I say, "Lola,
you'll only get glasses
if you really,
really need them."

And Lola says,
"But I DO
really need them...

... and I cannot see
my yellow toothbrush...

"... because I cannot
see that pink cookie...

.. and now I can
definitely not see at all."

So I say,
"That's because it is dark."

And Lola says,
"Oh, yes! But when I get
my new glasses,
I'll be able to see
in the dark."

I say,
"No you won't, Lola."

But Lola says,
"I will, Charlie! I will!"

The next day,
     Lola asks Mini,
"Can I try on
     your glasses?"

But Mini says,
"The glasses lady
     told me it's not
a good idea
because everyone's eyes
     are different.
     My glasses might
make your eyes
     a bit achy."

So Lola asks,
"But how will I
    know which glasses
will look nice on me?"

Mini says,
"Oh, that's easy.
        At the optician's,
you try on lots of glasses
        to see what
            you like best!"

And Lola shouts,
        "I can't wait!
    I can't wait!"

Later, Lola and I go to the Optician's.

Lola looks at all the different glasses.

When it's her turn to see the Optician, Lola says, "See you later, Charlie... with my glasses!"

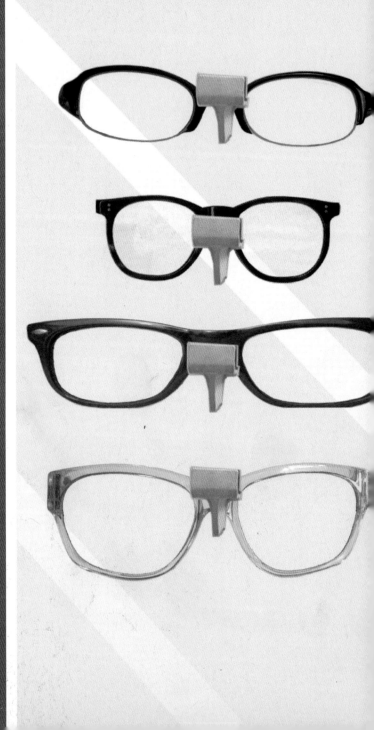

On the way home,
    Lola says,
"The **eye** test lady said
    I absolutely do not
need **glasses**, Charlie."

So I say,
    "That's good!
It means your **eyes**
    are very strong."

    And Lola says,
"But I really, really
    wanted **glasses**."

Then I say,
    "I have an idea!"

Lola and I
cut, paste and colour
pieces of paper.

We sprinkle **glitter**,
stick on **sparkly** stars,
and add **squiggly** lines
until we make...
the absolutely
most PERFECT pair
of **glasses**.

At school, Lola wears her new **glasses**.
Lotta has made some, too!
Mini says, "I like your **glasses**, Lola."
And Lola says, "Yes, **glasses** can be fun even
if you don't need them!"